GRIMMY™: FRIENDS DON'T LET FRIENDS OWN CATS!

GRIMMY™: FRIENDS DON'T LET FRIENDS OWN CATS!

by Mike Peters

TOR®

A TOM DOHERTY ASSOCIATES BOOK

NEW YORK

GRIMMY: FRIENDS DON'T LET FRIENDS OWN CATS!

TM and Copyright © 1996 by Grimmy, Inc.

A Tor Book
Published by Tom Doherty Associates, Inc.
175 Fifth Avenue
New York, N.Y. 10010

Tor Books on the World Wide Web:
http://www.tor.com

Tor® is a registered trademark of Tom Doherty Associates, Inc.

Library of Congress Cataloging-in-Publication Data

Peters, Mike
[Mother Goose & Grimm.   Selections]
Grimmy : friends don't let friends own cats / by Mike Peters.
p.   cm.
"A Tom Doherty Associates book."
ISBN 0-312-86068-4
I. Title.
PN6728.M67P474   1996
741.5973—dc20   95-52239
                          CIP

First Edition: August 1996

Printed in the United States of America

0   9   8   7   6   5   4   3   2

To the hard-working staff at the Grimmy Studio—
Rebecca, Ginger, Mary, Ben & Marci.

BABY NAMES FOR WEATHERMEN

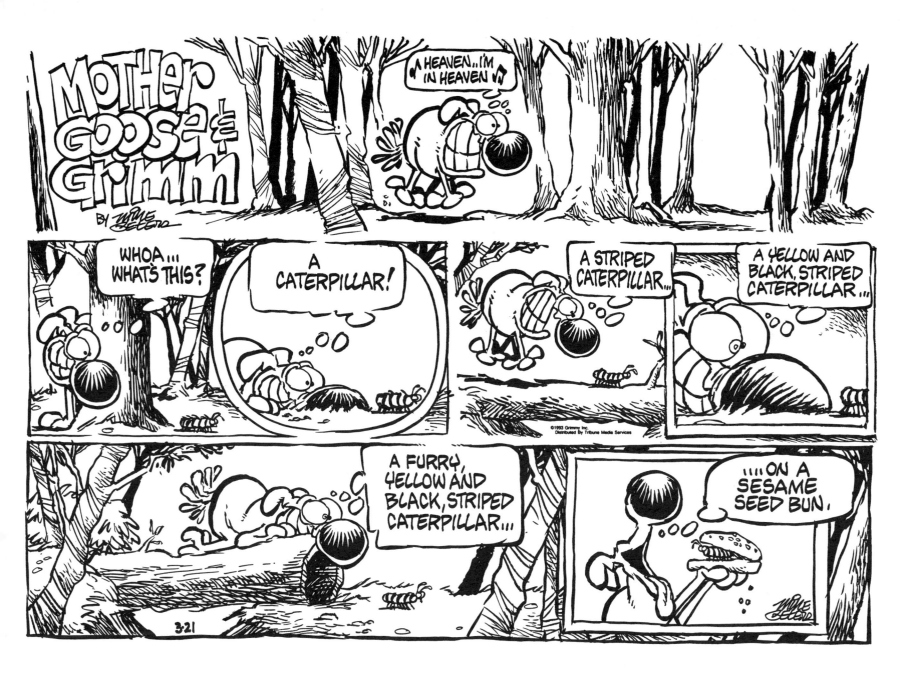

GRIMMY, STICK YOUR HEAD BACK IN....

Mother Goose & Grimm

WOOLSTOCK

HOW DEVILS LOSE THEIR JOBS

BOO!

ATTILA, WE NEED TO TRUST EACH OTHER MORE.

WE NEED TO BUILD ON OUR RELATIONSHIP.

I KNOW A LITTLE EXERCISE THAT CAN HELP US DO THAT...

ALL YOU HAVE TO DO IS IS STAND UP STRAIGHT AND TURN AROUND...

NOW SHUT YOUR EYES, FALL BACKWARDS AND WAIT FOR ME TO CATCH YOU...

DON'T WORRY, THIS IS A SIMPLE 10 STEP PROCESS.

CRASH

THAT'S STEP ONE, STEP TWO, STEP THREE...

THUD THUD

©1993 Grimmy Inc.
Distributed By Tribune Media Services

10-5

BENJI JUMPING.

NOT HERE, MY WIFE HAS EYES IN THE BACK OF HER HEAD.

10-6

DOCTOR, WE'D BETTER STOP GIVING GRIMMY THOSE **IRON** PILLS.

10-7

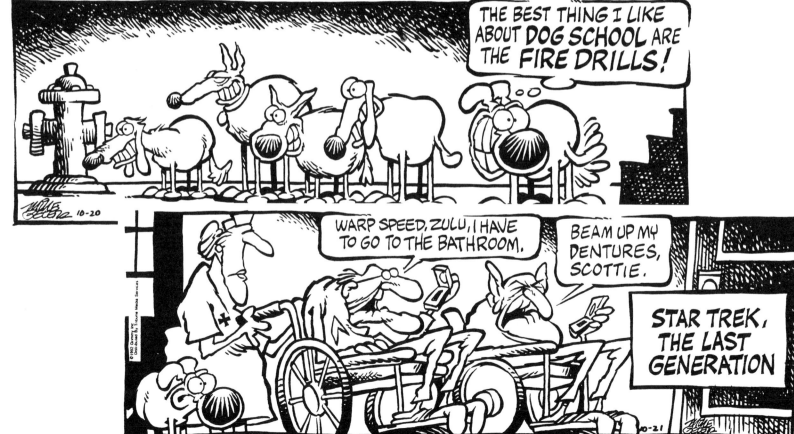

HOUDINI TRYING TO GET OUT OF HIS LEASE

MOTHER GOOSE & GRIMM

BY MIKE PETERS

MOTHER GOOSE AND SPACE DOG OF THE 21ST CENTURY

SPACEDOG LEAVES THE SAFETY OF THE SHUTTLE TO DO SOME NEEDED REPAIRS.

FORTUNATELY HIS GAS PROPELLED JET PACK ENABLES SPACE DOG TO MOVE AROUND FREELY...

FLOATING HUNDREDS OF MILES ABOVE THE EARTH IN ZERO GRAVITY.

HE FIRES HIS JET PACK TO HELP MANEUVER TO THE LEFT, THEN TO THE RIGHT...

THEN ANOTHER BURST PROPELS HIM CLOSER TO THE MOTHER SHIP.

EACH TIME MANEUVERING EFFORTLESSLY WITH LITTLE, TINY BURSTS OF GAS...

SNIFF,... GRIMMY!

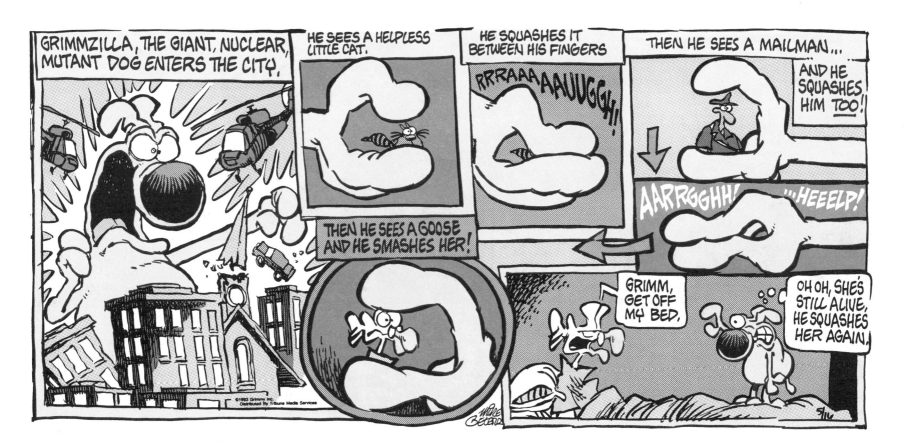

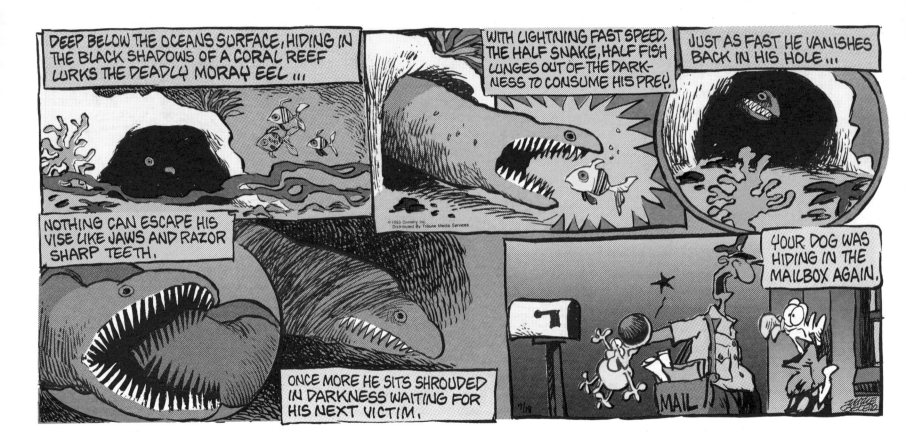

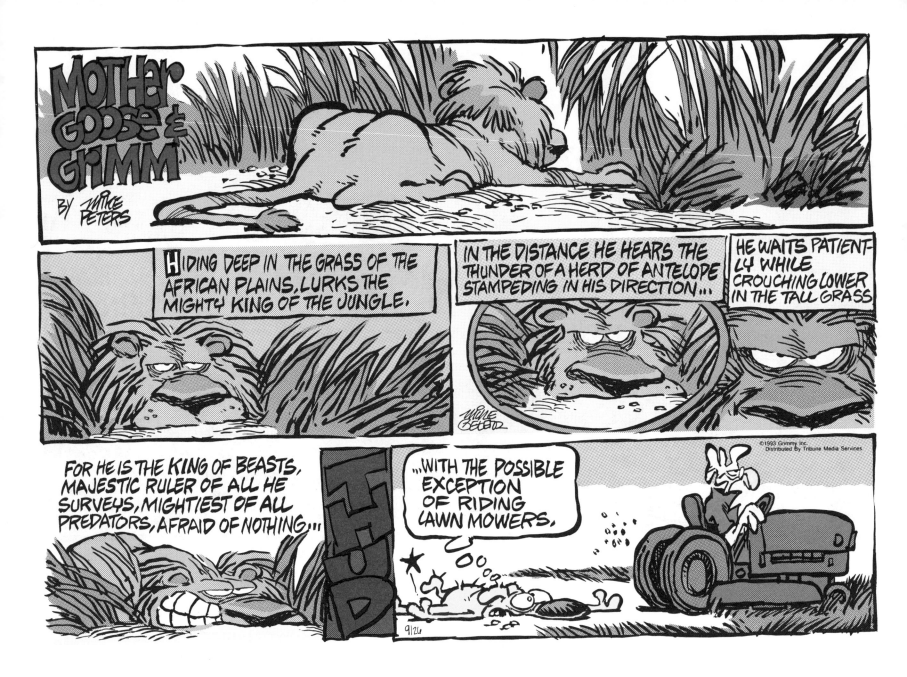

THE GUY WHO INVENTED VOICE MAIL

ELVIS SIGHTING #147

3-24

3/25

BEETHOVEN COMPOSING

BEETHOVEN DECOMPOSING

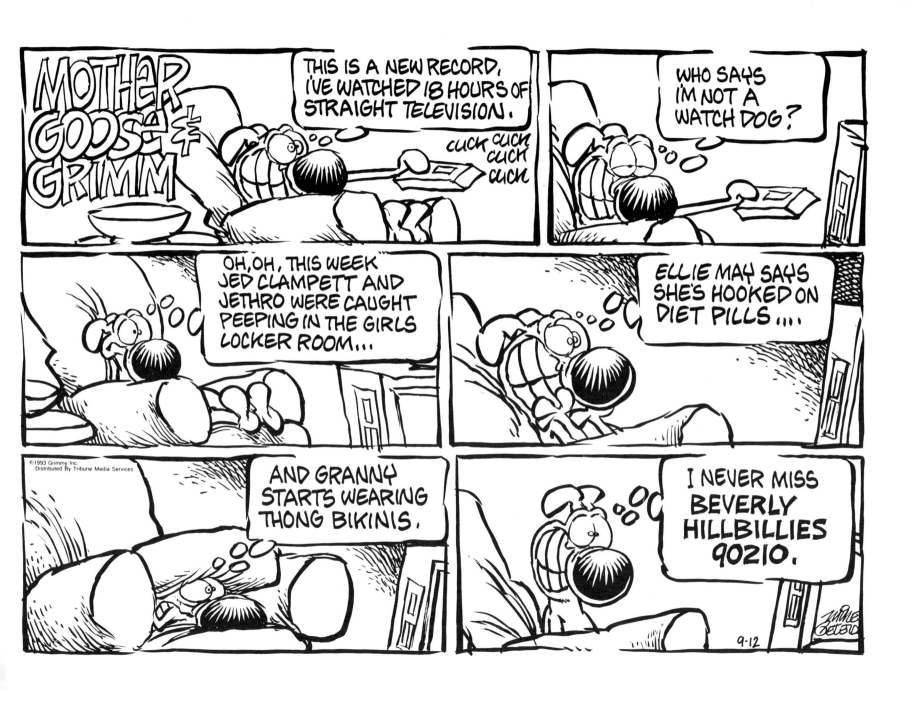

MORNING AT SALVADOR DALI'S

GUY LURES

SISKEL AND EBERT IN HELL

WHY THE INVISIBLE MAN
SELDOM EATS OUT

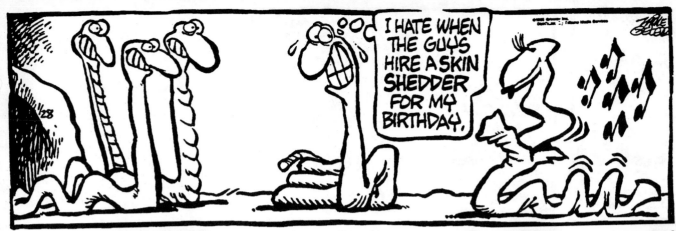

CARMEN MIRANDA RIGHTS

CLOWN FUNERALS

SOON AFTER THE SOVIET UNION DISNEYLAND BROKE UP INTO SEPARATE REPUBLICS.

CALL OF THE WILD WAITING

OPRAH INTERVIEWS PINOCCHIO

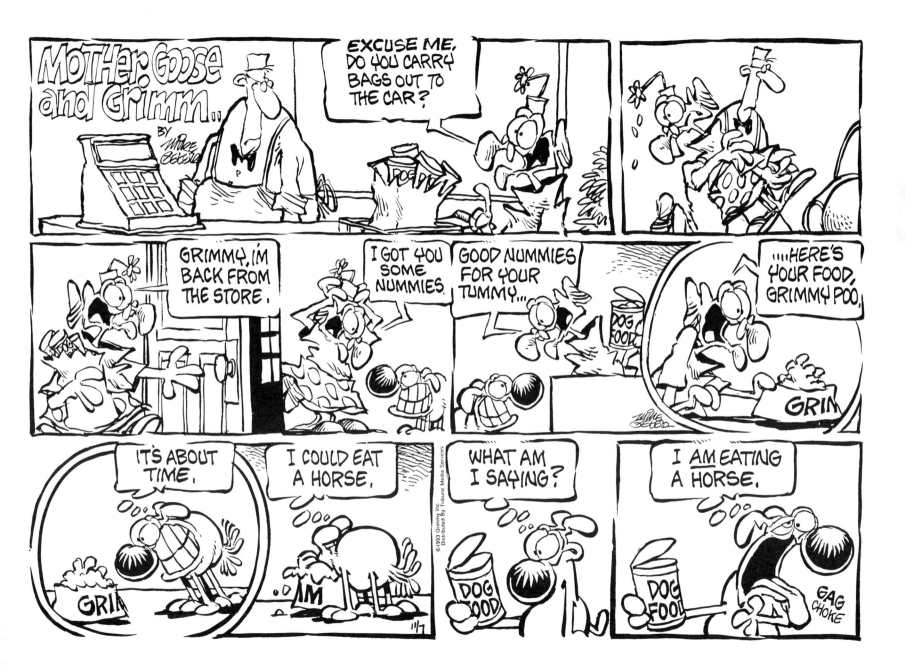

NIGHT OF THE LIVING BRAS

GOLDILOCKS AND THE THREE HINDUS

WHAT POODLES DO WHILE YOU'RE ASLEEP.